D.JUDE.MILLER
publishing

presents

EVERYBODY WAKE UP!!

written & illustrated
by
Daniel Jude Miller

Count to ten!
Find the hidden numbers
on the WAKE UP pages!

The sun arrived very early and sent
its warm rays out in every possible direction.
Some of those rays went through the window
of a cute little girl resting snug in her bed.

When the light gently brushed against
her cheek, she knew that it was
time to rise and shine.
It was time to wake up!

Sunny greeted the new day with a great big stretch and an even bigger smile. It was time to get started and today was going to be amazing!

She slipped on her favorite dress, combed her golden curls and grabbed her book bag. Now she was ready for another beautiful morning.

On the way to the kitchen, Sunny passed her little sister's room. The tiny baby was curled up under her blanket, surrounded by toys and sleeping peacefully.

"Babies sleep way too much," she thought.
"They miss out on all the best parts of the day!"
Sunny grabbed hold of the crib, took a
deep breath and shouted...

EVERYBODY

Sunny skipped down the hall and discovered her Mommy and Daddy still in bed. They looked comfortable but were snoring too loudly to hear the birds outside.

"Uh oh," she worried. "Their alarm clock must have broken. They're going to be late for work." Sunny leaned close to her father, took a deep breath and exclaimed...

As Sunny continued on, she realized that the triplets were still missing. When she searched their room, she found all three under the covers, ignoring the daylight.

"This isn't good," she declared.
"The school bus could be here any minute and they wouldn't want to miss it." Sunny tiptoed inside, took a deep breath and hollered...

Sunny hopped down the stairs but stopped short when she found all the family pets unaware that the sun had risen. The dog and the fish were in dreamland and the cats were both snoozing.

"It's almost 8 o'clock," she gasped.
"It's time to run and chase and jump!"
Sunny shut her eyes tight,
took a deep breath and yelled...

Before heading out to school, Sunny spent some time exploring in the garden. Right there under a big rock were all sorts of bugs that failed to hear the rooster crow.

"What a shame," she whispered. "There are so many pretty flowers to smell. Why should butterflies have all the fun?" Sunny bent close to the ground, took a deep breath and screeched...

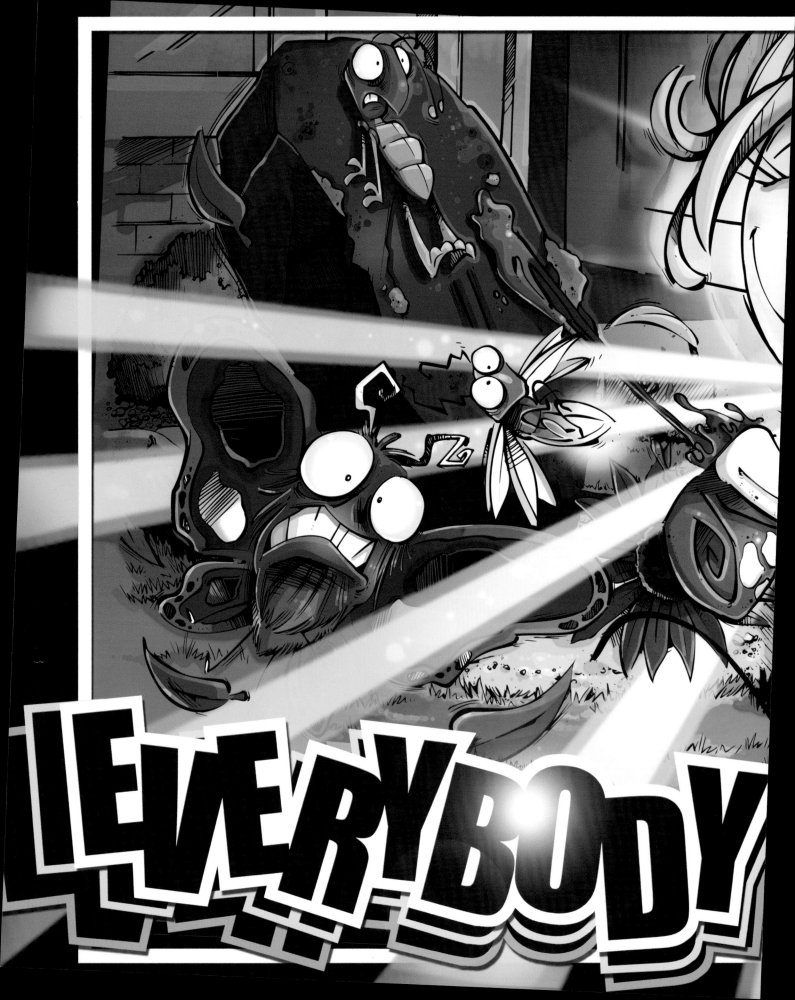

At school, Sunny noticed a kindergarten class where the children were supposed to be alert. Surprisingly, their books were shut, their pencils were still and their heads were down.

"This is silly," she chuckled. "How can you learn
anything with your eyes closed?"
Sunny crept up to the door,
took a deep breath and announced...

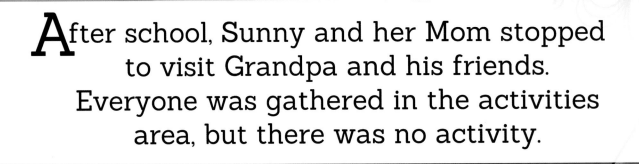

After school, Sunny and her Mom stopped to visit Grandpa and his friends. Everyone was gathered in the activities area, but there was no activity.

"What time is it?" Sunny teased.
"It's play time!"
She marched to the center of the room,
took a deep breath and howled...

Sunny's Mom wanted to check on her brother who worked at the movie theater. While they were chatting, Sunny took a peek at what was playing and wasn't happy with what she saw.

"Oh my," she fretted.
"The film is almost over and everyone is about
to miss the ending." Sunny nibbled her candy,
took a deep breath and bellowed...

Sometimes it was nice to take a
shortcut through the zoo.
Most of the animals there were active and excited,
but the bats weren't enjoying the day at all.

"How sad," Sunny sighed. "Weather
as splendid as this should never, ever be wasted!"
She pressed her nose against the glass,
took a deep breath and cried...

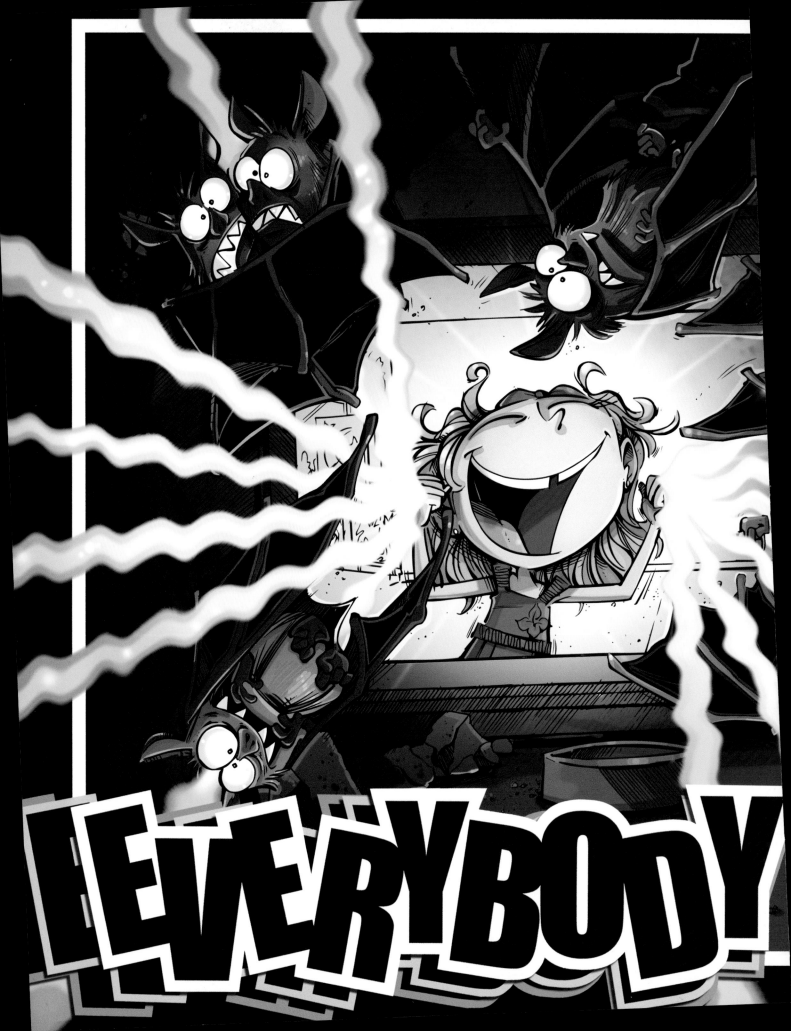

Two blocks from home, Sunny spotted a very quiet construction site. The equipment wasn't moving because the men were taking siestas right in the middle of their shifts!

"Is this normal?" Sunny questioned.
"Nothing will ever get built this way."
She picked up a megaphone,
took a deep breath and shrieked...

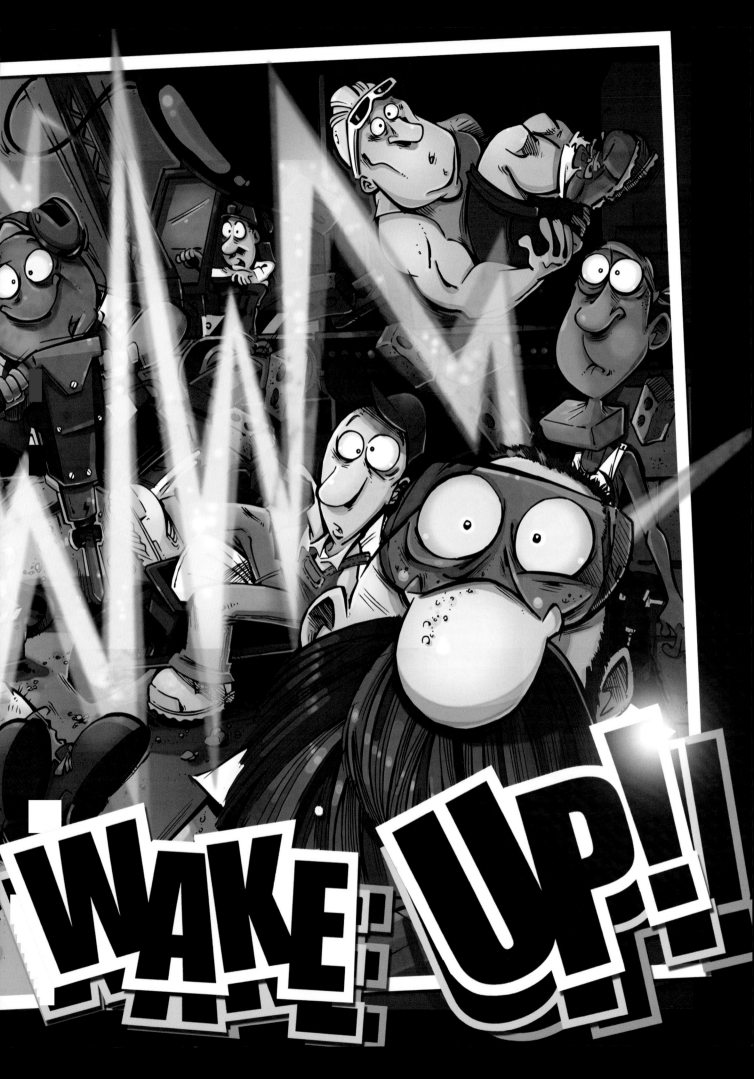

Later that evening, Sunny ate dinner, took a bath and brushed her teeth. She was exhausted from a long day and needed to rest for tomorrow.

She climbed into bed, pulled the sheets up to her chin and settled in for a good night's sleep. She had just drifted off when the door creaked open, there were deep breaths and...

Sunny just leaves people alone
when they're sleeping now.

Daniel Jude Miller

Dan does not endorse or encourage his readers to sneak
up to someone who is peacefully sleeping, anyone
who is calmly dreaming, individuals who are obviously in
a state of rest and shout abruptly, bang on metal objects
or howl in a wolf-like fashion.
No. Dan does not in any way wish to inspire
that type of behavior.

Although, he will laugh if he sees it!